D0106690

SKY H·I·G·H

BRAIN · BRAWN & BEYOND

THE JUNIOR NOVELIZATION

WALT DISNEY PICTURES PRESENTS "SKY HIGH" A GUNN FILMS PRODUCTION A MIKE MITCHELL FILM KELLY PRESTON
MICHAEL ANGARANO DANIELLE PANABAKER MARY ELIZABETH WINSTEAD AND KURT RUSSELL MUSIC SUPERVISOR LISA BROWN
MUSIC BY MICHAEL GIACCHINO COSTUME DESIGNER MICHAEL WILKINSON EDITED BY PETER AMUNDSON PRODUCTION DESIGNER BRUCE ROBERT HILL
DIRECTOR OF PHOTOGRAPHY SHELLY JOHNSON, A.S.C. EXECUTIVE PRODUCERS MARIO ISCOVICH ANN MARIE SANDERLN
PRODUCED BY ANDREW GUNN WRITTEN BY PAUL HERNANDEZ AND BOB SCHOOLEY & MARK McCORKLE DIRECTED BY MIKE MITCHELL

Skyhighmovie.com

Copyright © 2005 Disney Enterprises, Inc. All rights reserved under International and
Pan-American Copyright Conventions. Published in the United States by Random House
Children's Books, a division of Random House, Inc., New York, and simultaneously in Canada
by Random House of Canada Limited, Toronto, in conjunction with Disney Enterprises, Inc.
RANDOM HOUSE and colophon are registered trademarks of Random House, Inc.
Library of Congress Control Number: 2005921145   ISBN: 0-7364-2343-5

Printed in the United States of America   10 9 8 7 6 5 4 3 2 1

THE JUNIOR NOVELIZATION

Adapted by James Thomas

Based on the screenplay by Paul Hernandez and Bob Schooley & Mark McCorkle

Produced by Andrew Gunn

Directed by Mike Mitchell

Still photography by Sam Emerson and Suzanne Tenner

Random House 🏠 New York

FIFTEEN YEARS AGO . . .

The Commander and All-American Boy were trapped. Bound tightly in iron chains, the hero and his sidekick hung from the ceiling of an abandoned warehouse.

The Commander's huge muscles bunched as he used his superstrength against the chains. But it was no use.

They heard a harsh mechanical voice. "It would seem *I'm* in control, Commander. . . ."

Two villains, one dressed in techno-armor and a helmet, the other in a jester's outfit, stepped from the shadows.

"Royal Pain and Stitches!" the Commander said. "I should've known."

Royal Pain threw back his cape, revealing

a nasty-looking handheld cannon.

"The most brilliant invention of my career," said the mechanical villain. "The Pacifier!"

Stitches laughed maniacally for his master.

Royal Pain aimed the Pacifier at the Commander. "Prepare to be pacified!"

Suddenly a window on the other side of the room exploded. The high-flying heroine Jetstream rocketed in. She zipped behind the Commander's chains as Royal Pain blasted at her with the Pacifier. The energy beam shattered the chains, and the Commander dropped to the floor.

"Hold on!" shouted the Commander as he slammed his fists into the ground, sending a shock wave rippling through the room. Before Royal Pain could fire again, he was hurled against a hard stone wall. The Pacifier skidded across the floor.

The Commander and the dazed Royal Pain leapt for the gun. They arrived at the same moment.

"Let go!" Royal Pain said, pulling on one end of the gun. "You're going to break it!"

As the Commander pulled on the other end,

the stressed steel and plastic of the Pacifier began to crack. . . .

KA-BOOM!

On the other side of the room, Jetstream and All-American Boy held their breath, fearing the worst. They both sighed with relief as the Commander stepped through the smoke, the ruptured Pacifier thrown over one shoulder.

"Are you okay?" Jetstream asked.

"Better than Royal Pain," the Commander said.

On the scorched floor behind the Commander lay Royal Pain's smoldering helmet. The three heroes paused for a moment as they reflected on the villain's gruesome demise. Then the Commander turned to Jetstream and smiled.

"Coffee?" he asked brightly.

"I'd love to," Jetstream said, "but I have to get back to work. I'm selling my first house today."

"So you got a real estate cover, huh?" said the Commander. "I've been thinking of getting a new fake job. Mind if I tag along?"

Jetstream gave the Commander a big smile. "Not at all," she said.

Meanwhile, unnoticed by any of them, Stitches scurried away in the shadows with something clutched to his chest.

CHAPTER
1

Will Stronghold was nervous, and he had every reason to be. It was the first day of high school, and his powers still hadn't shown up.

Will lay back on his weight bench in the corner of his bedroom and glanced at the weights on the ends of the bar. He frowned. Even a normal kid should be able to lift that much, let alone a kid whose father was the mightiest superpowered hero on the planet!

Will took three quick breaths, closed his eyes, and . . . *pushed.*

He gasped in defeat and let his arms drop to his sides. He hadn't even been able to budge it.

A voice came from downstairs. "Will?"

It was his dad! Panicked, Will jumped to his

feet and struggled to throw more weight onto the bar. He could hear the sound of footsteps on the stairs.

"Come on, buddy, time to get moving."

Sweaty and out of breath, Will dropped back onto the bench. "Two hundred!" he gasped as his dad opened the door and walked in.

Will's dad was a big man. Broad-shouldered, with a narrow waist and a square chin, he looked like a comic book hero, which was just what he was. Most people knew Will's dad as Steve Stronghold, successful real estate agent, but Will knew him as the Commander.

"Oh, hey, Dad," Will said, sitting up. "Thought I'd get in a few sets before school."

The Commander smiled proudly as he glanced at the weight. He was wearing his horn-rimmed glasses, which did a remarkable job of keeping people from recognizing his true identity.

"Low weight, high reps," he said. "Good thinking. You don't want to bulk up."

Will nodded as he stretched his arms. "Yeah, I was going more for definition."

The Commander suddenly got serious as he sat down on the edge of the bed. "So, Will," he said. "I just wanted you to know how, um, proud I am that you'll be attending my alma mater. To think that someday you're going to follow me into the family business—"

"Real estate?" Will joked.

His father chuckled. He took off his glasses and slipped them into his shirt pocket, revealing the face that the public knew as the Commander's. "Right," he said with a wink. "Real estate."

The Commander picked up a forty-five-pound weight plate and flipped it in his fingers like a poker chip.

"Look," he said, a little nervously, "I know when you're a kid, you think your dad's invincible, and I nearly am. But who knows? Maybe next time I punch a meteor hurtling toward Earth, I'll be the one who shatters into a million pieces."

Will raised an eyebrow skeptically.

His father shrugged. "I guess what I'm trying to say is, it's nice to know that, whatever happens to me, you'll be around to save the world."

"Looking forward to it!" Will said.

His dad clapped him on the knee. Will cringed. As the Commander left, he tossed the forty-five-pound plate he'd been fiddling with to Will.

"Oof!" Will grunted as he caught it with both hands and flew back onto his bed.

When is my superstrength going to show up? he thought desperately.

▼

Downstairs, Will's best friend, Layla, had arrived. Layla dressed in long, flowing clothes that just screamed she was all about being environmentally friendly.

"Morning, Mrs. Stronghold," she said to Will's mom, who was busy putting breakfast on the table. Will's mom was a real estate agent, too. Wearing her tortoiseshell glasses, she was Josie Stronghold. Without them, she was the high-flying hero known as Jetstream!

"You hungry, Layla?" she asked. "I've got plenty of eggs, bacon—"

"No, thanks," Layla said. "I'm a vegetarian. You know how my mom can communicate with animals? Apparently they don't like being eaten."

Just then, Will's dad walked into the room.

"Good morning, Commander," Layla said.

"Commander?" said Will's dad, confused. Then he realized that his glasses were still in his shirt pocket. Quickly, he slipped them back on.

"Thanks, Layla," he said with a wink.

Will's mom was shaking her head. "I can't believe you and Will are starting high school. It seems like just yesterday you two were swimming naked in the kiddie pool."

"Mom!" Will said as he came in. To Layla he said, "It's like her power is to super-humiliate me!"

Just then, a cell phone rang. Will's dad pulled a red cell out of his pocket and flipped it open. "Uh-huh," he said into the phone. "I see. Thanks, Mayor."

Hanging up, he looked at Will's mom. "There's trouble downtown. Big trouble. A giant robot is attacking the freeway."

"Shoot!" said Will's mom. "And I really

wanted to see Will off to the bus."

She turned to Layla. "Remember the first day of preschool? He wouldn't let go of my leg—"

"Mom!" Will said.

With a grin Jetsteam quickly kissed Will on the cheek and darted out of the room.

The Commander clapped Will on the shoulder. Will smiled through the pain as his dad said, "Now, remember, Will. A lot of the kids at Sky High will only have one hero parent, not two. So take it easy on them. No showing off."

"Don't worry, Dad," Will said. "I'll try to keep the guns in their holsters."

Will's dad gave him a smile, then followed Jetstream out of the room.

Layla was looking at a few wilted plants behind the sink. "Looks like Jetstream's been too busy to feed you guys," she said to them.

Will grabbed his backpack. "Hey, she *has* saved your precious rain forest from total destruction like a dozen times."

Layla waved her hand over the plants. "I guess we can cut her some slack," she said as their flowers straightened and bloomed.

Will and Layla left the house and started down the street toward the bus stop. As they walked, they passed an ad for Will's parents' real estate company: IF IT'S STRONGHOLD, IT'S SOLD.

"I know it's just our first day," Layla was saying, "but I already can't wait to graduate and start saving mankind. And *woman*kind. And animalkind. And the rain forest, of course."

"Of course," Will said, poking her in the side to tease her.

Layla smiled, and Will smiled back.

You know, if she wasn't my oldest friend in the world . . . , Will thought.

Just then an ordinary-looking yellow school bus pulled to a stop next to them, and the doors folded open with a hydraulic *shunk!*

Will and Layla climbed the steps into the bus. The driver was wearing a plain blue baseball cap and a matching blue windbreaker. The kids on the bus were chatting and laughing and listening to music.

Will turned to the driver. "Uh, is this the bus to Sky High?"

"*Shhh!*" whispered the driver. He slammed the bus doors. "You want every villain in the neighborhood to know we're here?"

"Sorry," Will said.

"What's your name, freshman?" the bus driver asked.

"Will Stronghold," said Will.

The bus driver's eyes opened wide with appreciation. He turned in his seat and called back to the other kids, "It's Will Stronghold! The son of the Commander and Jetstream!"

The entire bus got quiet as every kid turned to stare at Will.

Great, thought Will. *So much for blending in.*

"I'm so sorry, sir," the bus driver said. "My name is Ron Wilson, Sky High bus driver. If there is anything I can do to make your journey more comfortable, please let me know."

Ron turned to the two kids sitting in the seat right behind him. "You two, get up!" he said. "The seat behind me is reserved for Will Stronghold."

A nerdy-looking boy immediately began stuffing his books into his Commander and Jetstream backpack.

"It would be an honor!" the boy said.

"That's okay," said Will. "You really don't have to—"

"I *want* to," the boy said. He held up one of his books. "Chapter two of the school handbook. Your grandfather was one of the founders of Sky High. You're third generation!"

The boy stuffed the handbook into his bag and turned to his seatmate, a funky-looking girl with purple hair and a frown across her face.

"Come on, Magenta," the boy said. "Get up."

"Come on yourself, Ethan," the girl said, scowling. "Why do I have to get up? He only needs one seat."

"So he can sit with his girlfriend," Ethan said.

"Girlfriend?" Will said. He laughed nervously. "Who, Layla? We've been friends since forever."

"Yeah, totally," Layla said. "He's like my brother."

A slight boy wearing glasses leaned across the aisle. "In that case, hi," he said to Layla, giving her a way-too-friendly smile. "I'm Larry."

"Come on, Layla," Will said. "We'll just find a seat in the back."

"Hey, Will! Layla! What's up?" called a cocky-looking kid with spiky blond hair.

"Zach," Will said as he and Layla sat down next to him. "How was your summer?"

"To be honest, it was tough, man," Zach said. "Tough. I mean, I was seriously sweating it, listening to my dad going, 'I powered up before I started shaving!' and here's me, halfway through August, and zip!"

Will lowered his voice. "So you haven't gotten your powers?" he asked hopefully.

Zach looked shocked. "Dude, you think I'd even show up today if *that* happened? Nope, woke up a few weeks ago and *bam!*"

He grinned smugly, turning his profile from side to side as if reporters were already snapping his photograph for saving the world.

"Oh . . . that's great," Will said, trying to hide his disappointment. Layla gave him a close look.

"So what is it? Your power?" Will asked.

"Easy, cowboy," Zach said. "You'll have to wait and see like everybody else. But it's awesome, man! And come on, it's not like you've ever powered up in front of us. Tell you what . . . I'll show you my power if you show me yours."

The kids in the seats around them got quiet. Will laughed nervously. "Don't we have anything better to talk about than superpowers?" he asked.

The kids glanced at one another uncertainly. Finally, deciding that Will was joking, they started to laugh. Will joined in, relieved.

Layla was the only one not laughing.

Ron the bus driver closed the doors after the last kid got on the bus.

"That's everyone!" Ron said.

Putting down his clipboard, he took off his cap and replaced it with one that said SKY HIGH across the front. From the arm of his windbreaker, he ripped a patch. Underneath it was a logo that showed a stylized young hero encircled by atomic bands.

"Next stop," Ron called back, "Sky High!"

CHAPTER 2

Picking up speed, the bus darted through traffic and down a deserted off-ramp. Bars snapped down across the kids' laps, and seat belts shot out of the seats, strapping them in tightly.

"Hang on!" Ron shouted. "We're going off road!"

The bus roared up a street with a ROAD CLOSED sign. Ron hit a button on the dash, and the sign folded down. Then, as they approached a ROAD ENDS sign, it tilted back into a ramp. The bus charged up the ramp and shot into the air.

The kids screamed as the bus sprouted wings and jet engines. The engines ignited with a roar and the bus flew into the sky.

The bus gained altitude and popped through

the clouds. Ahead, the kids could see their destination—Sky High. The entire campus—buildings, playing fields, stadium—sat upon a massive floating platform like some futuristic city in the clouds.

The kids fell into a stunned silence.

"There she is," Ron said. "Sky High. Kept aloft by the latest in antigravitational propulsion. She is in constant motion as a precaution against those who might have nefarious plans, her location supplied to only a handful of qualified individuals like myself, Ron Wilson, bus driver."

Ron gently landed the bus and opened the doors. As the kids filed off, he said, "Word of advice: don't miss the bus, 'cause the bus waits for no one. Except for you, Will."

Ron handed Will his business card. It said RON WILSON, BUS DRIVER.

"Thanks, Ron," Will said, slipping the card into his wallet and jumping off the bus.

Will looked around in awe. Two girls chatted as they flew slowly past the flagpole. On the ground two guys were following a pretty girl with an armload of books. One of the guys pointed his finger and zapped her with a burst of electricity.

The girl dropped her books in surprise, and the guys laughed. The girl spun around and blasted the guy who'd shocked her with a freeze ray. The guy turned into a human-sized block of ice.

Cool, Will thought.

Then a giant cheerleader pyramid appeared out of nowhere. All the cheerleaders looked exactly the same!

"Hello, freshmen, don't be shy!" chanted the cheerleaders. "Welcome, newbies, to Sky High! Juniors, seniors, all the rest, we're back to school, Sky High's the best!"

The pyramid shrank down into a single cheerleader. "We're number one!" she cried, giving the air a spunky high kick.

The next thing Will knew, he and the rest of the freshmen were surrounded by a blur. It forced them into a tighter and tighter group.

The blur stopped and became an upper classman guy.

"Your attention, please!" the upperclassman

said. He stepped aside as another upperclassman came down the school steps.

"I'm Lash," he said. He pointed at the first upperclassman. "This is Speed. As representatives of the Sky High Welcoming Committee, we'd like to say . . . you're all tools."

Speed laughed obnoxiously. "He's kidding, fresh meat. But if you'll form a line, we'll be happy to collect the fifteen-dollar new student fee."

Lash stretched out an elastic arm, palm up, across the lawn. It stopped in front of Ethan, the nerdy boy who'd wanted to give Will his seat on the bus. The fingers waggled for a moment.

"Um, there was nothing about a new student fee in the handbook," Ethan said.

In a flash, Lash's arm retracted, bringing Lash himself right into the kid's face.

Lash didn't look happy.

"Okay, guys," someone said. "Very funny. I'll take it from here."

Will turned to find the most beautiful girl he'd ever seen walking across the lawn toward them.

"Hi, everybody," the girl said. "I'm Gwen

Grayson, your student body president."

Gwen caught Will's eye and gave him a dazzling smile. Will felt like he'd been hit by a truck. Gwen's words became a meaningless buzz as he watched her flip her honey-brown hair over her shoulder.

Layla elbowed him in the ribs.

". . . and if you can just remember those three simple rules," Gwen was saying, "I guarantee you won't fall off the edge of the school."

"Rules?" Will mumbled. He turned to Layla, who was glaring at him. "What rules?"

"Weren't you paying attention?" Layla asked sarcastically.

"Oh. *Those* rules," Will said.

The new students filed into the building. Each was given a name tag before they were led to the gym. One entire wall of the gym was a massive window. Outside, huge clouds floated by silently.

Will heard a low roar behind him and then a loud *whoosh!* The freshmen ducked as a fiery comet shot over their heads and careened around the room. The ball of fire came to a stop at a podium and transformed into a stern-looking older woman.

"Good morning. I'm Principal Powers," the woman said. "On behalf of all the faculty and staff, welcome to Sky High.

"You are now part of the most unique high school in the world. Founded in nineteen fifty-one to deal with the postwar hero baby boom, our mission is to mold today's students into tomorrow's heroes. Sky High graduates have gone on to apprehend sixty-two of the world's most dangerous supervillains, thwart twenty-seven alien invasions, and stop three out of the four mutants who have run for president."

Everyone cheered.

"A few minutes from now, you'll go through power placement, and your own heroic journey will begin."

Will tuned out of the principal's speech. "'Power placement'?" he whispered to his friends.

"Sounds fascist," said Layla.

Ethan leaned in. "Power Placement, chapter nine," he said. "It's how they decide where you go."

"The hero track or the loser track," said

Ethan's seatmate from the bus, the girl with the purple hair and bad attitude, Magenta.

"There's a loser track?" Will asked, feeling panic beginning to rise.

Zach snorted. "They can call it whatever they want, but if you don't make hero, then you're just a sidekick."

"Uh, the preferred term is 'hero support,'" Ethan said.

"And this test is today?" Will asked, definitely starting to panic.

Magenta glared at him impatiently. "Weren't you listening to a word Gwen was saying?"

"What are you worried about?" Zach asked. "You're a Stronghold. You'll rule."

"And may I say," Principal Powers continued, "it's so nice to see the talents of our most prestigious alumni carried on in our latest class of heroes. I'm sure we won't be disappointed."

Principal Powers was looking right at Will.

"And now," the principal said, "to the board of ed meeting!"

The principal morphed back into a ball of fire

and roared over the kids' heads and out of the room.

The kids watched her go, then turned to find a platform rising out of the gym floor. Beside the platform stood a muscular man carrying a clipboard and wearing a whistle around his neck.

"All right, listen up!" the big man said. "My name is Coach Boomer. You may know me as Sonic Boom. You may not. Regardless, here's how power placement is going to work."

The coach pointed to the platform. "You will step up here and show me your power. And, yes, you will do so in front of the entire class. I will then decide where you will be assigned, hero or sidekick."

Will started to feel as if he might get sick.

The coach scanned the group. "Now, every year there are a few students—or, as I like to call them, whiner babies—who feel the need to complain about their placement. Let's get one thing straight: my word is law. My judgment is final. Are we clear?"

The kids looked at one another nervously.

"I said," the coach roared, "ARE WE CLEAR?"

The coach's shout sent sonic ripples pulsing across the gym. The kids plugged their ears as the basketball backboard above them shattered.

As one they shouted, "Yes, Coach Boomer!"

The coach nodded. "Let's not make Coach Boomer raise his voice again."

The coach pointed his clipboard at the tiny kid who'd introduced himself to Layla on the bus.

"You!" the coach said. "What's your name?"

"L-L-Larry," the kid said, terrified.

"Little Larry, get up here. NOW."

As Larry slowly climbed onto the platform, Layla turned to Will. "What's humiliating him in front of everyone going to prove? This is so unfair!"

They watched as Larry removed his glasses and closed his eyes. Suddenly the tiny boy transformed into a stone-skinned giant.

The coach wasn't impressed. "Car!" he called out.

From the ceiling directly above the platform dropped a car. Larry caught it easily and put it down on its tires.

The coach made a note on his clipboard. "Big Larry," he said, jerking his head toward the area where he wanted the heroes to stand. "Hero!"

Larry beamed with pride. The entire gym shook as he stepped down from the platform and walked to the "hero" side of the bleachers. Behind him the car was retracted to the ceiling.

"Okay, so he's good," Zach said. "But I'm better." Zach bounded onto the platform.

"The name's Zach, Coach Boomer," Zach said. "Try not to drop your clipboard."

The class watched as Zach cracked his neck, then his knuckles. He stretched one arm, then the other, then jumped up and down in place.

"Any day now, superstar," said Coach Boomer.

"I'm doing it," Zach said.

"Doing what?" asked the coach.

"I'm glowing," said Zach.

"I don't think so," the coach said.

"Well, it's easier to see in a dark room," said Zach. "Maybe we could turn off the lights, or you could cup your hands around your eyes and get up real close—"

"Sidekick," said the coach, making a note on his clipboard.

"Are you sure you don't want to just turn off the lights?" Zach asked.

"SIDEKICK!" the coach boomed. The sonic wave knocked Zach right off the platform.

The coach pointed at Ethan. "You! Front and center!"

As Ethan walked over to the platform, he said, "Coach, I'd like to begin by saying what an honor it is to—"

"Is that your power?" Coach Boomer asked. "Butt-kissing?"

"No, sir," Ethan said, chuckling. "Very funny, sir. I'd heard you had a wicked sense of humor, but I—"

"Shut up and power up!" the coach interrupted.

"Right away, sir!" said Ethan, melting. Literally. Ethan became a puddle of goo.

"Say, that's pretty impressive," said the coach. "For an ice cream cone. Sidekick!"

Over the next few hours, Will watched as

student after student showed off one amazing superpower after another. One boy could sprout four extra arms.

"Hero," pronounced Coach Boomer. "And see me about the wrestling team."

A girl jumped into the air, tucked up her legs, and turned into a bouncing ball.

"Sidekick!" said the coach, kicking the ball into the bleachers.

Then it was Magenta's turn.

"Let me guess," the coach said. "You have the power to turn your hair the ugliest shade of purple I've ever seen."

"Yeah, ha ha ha," said Magenta. "I'm a shape-shifter."

"So what's your shtick?" the coach asked. "Rhino? Tiger? Swarm of killer bees?"

"Actually . . . ," Magenta said. With a flash she morphed into a small purple guinea pig.

"Guinea pig?" the coach asked incredulously. "Not even a *swarm* of guinea pigs? Sidekick!"

The coach scanned the remaining students. Only Will, Layla, and a few others were left.

The coach pointed at Layla. "You! Flower child! Let's go!"

Layla glanced at Will, then said, "I believe powers should only be used when the situation demands it."

"Well, you're in luck," said Coach Boomer. "This is the situation, and I'm demanding it."

Layla raised her voice so that everyone could hear her. "To participate in this test would be to support a flawed system. I think the whole hero/sidekick dichotomy only serves to—"

"Let me get this straight," Coach Boomer interrupted. "Are you refusing to show me your powers?"

All the students covered their ears.

"Well, it's a lot more complicated than that," Layla said. "I mean—"

"SIDEKICK!" the coach boomed.

Layla's flowing clothes fluttered as the sonic wave blew past her.

The coach looked at Will. Suddenly Will wished he had Ethan's power and could melt into a puddle on the floor.

Just as Coach Boomer was pointing at him, the bell rang.

"We'll pick it up right after lunch," Boomer said. He looked meaningfully at Will. "Starting with you."

CHAPTER 3

Will followed the others to the cafeteria. After piling food onto trays, they started looking for seats.

Will bumped into a big tough-looking kid. "Sorry about that," Will said.

The big kid just glared.

Will, Layla, Zach, and Ethan found a free table and sat down. Will looked up to find the kid he'd bumped into sitting nearby.

"Okay, am I crazy," Will asked, "or is that guy staring at me?"

Zach glanced over. "Oh, man. Dude."

"What?" Will asked.

"That's Warren Peace," Zach said.

Layla's eyes went wide. "*That's* Warren Peace?

I've heard of him. Mom's a hero, Dad's a villain. *Major* issues."

"So?" asked Will. "Where do I come in?"

"If I may?" Ethan said. "Your dad busted his dad."

Will shook his head. "Great. First day of Sky High and I already have an archenemy."

The kids ate quickly and dumped their trays. On their way out, Will accidentally bumped into Gwen.

"Oh!" Will said. "I'm—"

"Will Stronghold," Gwen said.

"You know my name?" Will asked.

Gwen grinned. "Name tag."

Will glanced down at the name tag on his shirt and mentally kicked himself.

"Right," he said. "Uh, these are my friends, Zach and—"

"Layla. Got it. I'm Gwen," she said. "So how's power placement going?"

Will put on a fake smile. "So far, so good," he said.

"Not surprised!" said Gwen. "Listen, I need a

freshman rep for the Homecoming committee. If you're interested, we can talk about it over lunch sometime."

"I eat lunch!" Will blurted out.

Gwen laughed. To Layla she said, "How cute is he? Well, I'll see you guys around."

Trying to avoid embarrassing himself yet again, Will hurried to the gym while his friends went to find their lockers. He had to talk to the coach.

None of the other students were there yet. Coach Boomer was standing on the platform, polishing his whistle.

"Uh, Coach?" Will said. "Can I talk to you?"

"Steve Stronghold's boy, right?" the coach asked. "Just like your old man, always first back from lunch. I remember this one time he—"

The bell rang, and the other students started coming back into the gym.

"Right," Coach Boomer said, watching the class come in. "So, what'd you want to tell me?"

Will grimaced. Quickly, he whispered into the coach's ear.

The coach recoiled. "What do you mean

you don't know what your power is?"

The rest of the class fell silent, staring at Will.

The coach suddenly smiled. "Oh, I got ya. Messing around with the coach. Just like your old man. CAR!"

Will dropped to the ground as the car landed on top of him. When it retracted back into the ceiling, he popped to his feet.

"Are you insane?" he said. "I don't have superstrength!"

For a moment the coach was perplexed; then his face cleared. "So you're a flier, huh? Just like your mom. Why didn't you say so?"

The coach pressed a button, and the floor under Will sprang up. Will went flying into the air and slammed into a wall. He slid to the floor, dazed.

"Kid, stop messing around," said the coach. "I don't have all day. What's your power?"

Will was holding his aching head. "I . . . don't . . . have . . . one," he groaned.

The coach crossed his arms, stunned. Then he came to a decision. "STRONGHOLD: SIDEKICK!"

The coach's words thundered throughout the

school. At the back of the gym, Lash and Speed stopped stuffing a freshman into a garbage can long enough to snicker. In the hall outside the gym, Gwen and the multiplying cheerleader, Penny, were standing in front of a mirror, trying on different shades of lipstick. The shock wave reached them, and the mirror cracked. Gwen and Penny looked at each other in surprise.

The shock wave reached the principal's office. Looking concerned, she caught a flower vase as it jumped off her desk.

In front of the school, Ron the bus driver had just finished polishing the windows in the door of the bus. The shock wave smacked into him and shattered the glass.

Will was sitting in the nurse's office, an ice bag on his head. Nurse Spex tapped his knee with a rubber hammer, and his leg jerked slightly.

"I remember doing this to your father when he was your age," the nurse said. "He kicked me right through that wall!"

"You haven't called him yet, have you?" Will asked nervously.

Nurse Spex laughed. "Yeah, like I want to be the one who tells the Commander his son has no powers."

Will's face fell.

"I just can't believe you managed to keep it from him so long," the nurse said.

Will shrugged. "I sawed halfway through all our furniture. Every time he got suspicious, I just broke another chair."

Nurse Spex put on her stethoscope.

"Let's take a look at your chest," she said. She listened to Will's heart. Then she blinked twice and sent twin X-ray beams out of her eyes, revealing Will's heart and lungs. "Well, nothing seems to be broken," the nurse said, turning off her piercing gaze.

She made a note in a folder. "In fact, you're in perfect health."

"Except for the fact I have no powers," Will said glumly.

Nurse Spex sighed. "Maybe you're just a late bloomer. You could still get one—or both—of them, your mom's flying or your dad's superstrength."

"But *when?*"

"The kids who get bit by radioactive insects or fall in a vat of toxic waste, their powers usually show up the next day. Or they die," the nurse said thoughtfully. "But kids who inherit their powers? Impossible to say."

"But I *will* get them," Will insisted.

Nurse Spex took off her stethoscope and put it to the side. "Theoretically," she said.

"Theoretically?" Will cried.

Nurse Spex nodded. "There are cases—rare but not unheard of—where the child of superpowered parents never acquires any powers whatsoever."

"There are?" Will said.

"Well, only one that I know of," said the nurse. "You've met Ron Wilson, bus driver?"

Will glanced out the window to see Ron sweeping up the broken glass from the door. Thinking no one was looking, Ron hopped on the broom and pretended to ride it.

Will looked away, utterly depressed.

Late that afternoon, Will got home to find his

mom in the kitchen getting dinner ready. His dad was sitting at the table, playing with a beach ball-sized metallic eye from the giant robot he and Jetstream had destroyed that morning.

When Will walked in, his dad stood up and said, "Hey, Will! So how was your first day?"

Will took a deep breath. "Dad, we need to talk," he said.

"Oh, a little hero-to-hero talk," said Will's dad. "I know just the place."

He winked at Will's mom, tucked the robot eyeball under his arm, and led Will into the den.

"So here's the thing—" Will tried to explain.

"This isn't the place, Will," his father interrupted. With a sparkle in his eye, the Commander swung aside an oil painting, revealing a computerized touch screen.

Will suddenly realized what was going on. "The secret sanctum?" he asked.

His father nodded proudly. "Go ahead, son. I added your biometrics this morning."

Will hesitated. He knew he should say something and say it *now*. But his father was so proud. Slowly, Will reached for the touch screen.

"Just remember one thing," his father said. "You

must never bring anyone into the secret sanctum. That's why it's called the *secret* sanctum."

"I understand," Will said.

Will put his hand on the screen. It glowed and beeped a coded sequence, and then the cabinet next to it popped open. Behind the cabinet door were two poles. Together Will and his father slid down the poles into the secret sanctum.

Will looked around. It was an awesome room, with high-tech gadgetry built into almost every surface. But best of all . . .

"You've got a pool table!" Will said.

"And a pinball machine!" his father said proudly. It was a Commander and Jetstream model. Will's mom held the high score.

The Commander put down the robot eyeball, then started showing Will around. "Now, you've got your mom's stuff over here, your scientific equipment and whatnot . . . Will?"

Will was standing by a trophy wall, framed by a velvet curtain, where numerous prizes were lovingly hung and illuminated. Alien battle armor. A robotic insect. A titanium skull.

Will's dad came up beside him. "Our greatest battles," he said. "Our finest moments. Ticranium's head. Exo's bug-bots."

"Whoa!" Will said, pointing at one object in particular. He couldn't believe his eyes. "Is that—"

"Royal Pain's Pacifier," his dad said, taking it down off the shelf. "That was a great day, the first time your mother and I teamed up to fight evildoers. It's my proudest possession."

Will examined it closely. "It's incredible," he said. "What's it do?"

"No idea," his dad said with a shrug. He put the Pacifier back on the shelf and draped his arm over Will's shoulder.

"This wall tells our story, your mother and me," he said, "of kicking butt and taking names. But now it's time for a new chapter in the story. . . ."

Will's dad opened the velvet curtains a little more to reveal an empty portion of the trophy wall. At the bottom was a plate engraved with Will's name.

"The three of us," Will's dad went on, "fighting crime side by side by side."

Father and son stood together, staring at the empty portion of the trophy wall. Then Will's dad clapped him on the shoulder and said, "So, what'd you want to tell me?"

Will looked at his father's proud smile and said, "That I'm going to kick your butt in pool!"

His father laughed. "We'll see about that!"

Will's dad placed his palm on another touch screen, and a cabinet slid open to reveal a dozen pool cues.

"Choose your weapon, sir," Will's dad said.

As Will and his father talked and laughed, behind them, now forgotten, sat the staring robot eyeball . . . which was more than just an eyeball.

Royal Pain and Stitches were using a camera hidden in that eyeball to spy on the Commander and his son. In their secret lair, they watched on a viewscreen as Will prepared to break.

Stitches was practically jumping up and down. "You were right!" he said to Royal Pain. "He took it home!"

Royal Pain hit a button, and the picture zoomed in on the Commander.

"Of course he did," Royal Pain snapped. The voice was cold, calculating, and mechanical. "The man's got an ego the size of . . . well, a giant robot!"

Royal Pain fiddled with a lever, and the camera turned and zoomed in on the Pacifier. Stitches clapped his hands and cackled with glee.

CHAPTER 4

The next day, the pressure was off. For better or worse, the students knew where they stood.

Their first class of the morning was Hero Support. Will, Layla, Zach, Ethan, and Magenta were there, along with all the other sidekicks from power placement the day before.

The bell rang and in walked their teacher. He was a middle-aged man wearing a red sport coat, a blue tie, and khakis that barely reached around his sizable middle.

"Good morning, class," he said. "Welcome to Hero Support. My name is . . ."

Suddenly the man dove behind a screen and rolled out the other side in a spandex costume.

". . . All-American Boy!" he concluded.

The kids' jaws dropped. All-American Boy's costume might have fit fifteen years before, but now his cape was too short, his pants were too tight, and his form-fitting shirt didn't fit his form quite so well anymore.

"Today I go by Mr. Boy. And it's my privilege to help you become the best sidekicks—I mean, *hero support*—you can be."

"When do we pick our names and costumes?" Zach asked. "Because I call dibs on Zach Attack."

"You don't really get to pick," said Mr. Boy. "At graduation, you will be assigned to a hero and he or she will decide what you are called and what you wear. When I got paired with the Commander, red, white, and blue it was!"

"Excuse me," Will said. "You worked for the Commander?"

"*With* the Commander," Mr. Boy corrected. "Yes. We were a great team."

"But," Will said, confused, "I thought he just worked with Jetstream."

"And why is that, Mr. . . ." Mr. Boy checked his seating chart. ". . . Stronghold? *Stronghold?*"

Mr. Boy looked up at Will. "You're Steve's son?"

"Yup," Will said.

Mr. Boy looked hurt. "He's never mentioned me? Really?"

"Nope," Will admitted.

"Not a photo or a—"

"Sorry," said Will.

"Well, that makes sense," Mr. Boy said with a forced laugh. "It's not like the Commander has time to just sit around flipping through the old scrapbooks, which I made him. He's out there saving the world. With your mom."

Suddenly there was a huge explosion from outside the classroom.

"Incoming!" Mr. Boy cried.

The lights flickered and died, leaving the classroom in total darkness, except for the bright green glow coming from Zach.

"Aw, look," Magenta said. "He glows."

The door opened and a teacher came in. "Little misfire in the Mad Science Lab," the teacher said. "No need to panic."

The lights popped back on, revealing the

teacher to be the famous Medulla, with a brains-welled head the size of a globe.

"No, no, of course not, Mr. Medulla!" came Mr. Boy's voice. "We in Hero Support are trained not to panic."

Mr. Medulla and the students looked around for Mr. Boy and finally found him clinging to an overhead duct. With a creak, it bent and then crashed to the floor, taking Mr. Boy with it.

"A little help?" Mr. Boy moaned.

For the next several days, Will and his friends went from class to class, learning how to be good sidekicks and getting used to the school. Despite himself, Will started to enjoy it.

One evening the gang was over at Will's house, studying together. They were sprawled around the living room as Will read from a textbook.

"A radioactive zombie is charging at your hero. Do you hand him (A) his silver-tipped crossbow, (B) a wooden spike, (C)—"

"That's so weak," Zach said. "I'm already

holding the crossbow; why can't I just kill the zombie myself?"

"'Cause we're hero support," Ethan replied. "And if your hero asks for a crossbow, you hand it to him."

"Or *her*," Layla said.

"By the way, Zach," Ethan said. "You can't kill a zombie. You can only *re*kill him."

"Or *her*," Layla said again.

Then from the kitchen they heard Will's dad's voice. "If you kids are all in here, who's out there saving the world?"

The kids all looked up as the Commander, decked out in his full uniform, walked in.

Will sat up straight, suddenly very nervous. "Dad, why are you home so early?"

The Commander waved his hand dismissively. "Eh, after I stopped the Superdome from collapsing, I decided not to stick around for the rest of the game."

He glanced around the room. "I see you and Layla have made some new friends."

Ethan stepped forward and enthusiastically

stuck out his hand. "It's an honor to meet you, Commander."

They shook hands. Ethan winced, but only slightly.

"What's your name, what's your power?" the Commander asked.

"I'm Ethan, sir," Ethan said, "and I melt."

"Okay," the Commander said, nonplussed.

"Zach. I glow," said Zach.

"I see," said the Commander.

"Magenta," Magenta said. "I shape-shift."

"Oh?" the Commander asked, impressed.

"Into a guinea pig," Magenta concluded.

"Oh," said the Commander, less impressed. He shrugged and smiled. On his way out, he said, "Well, nice to have met everyone."

Later, when Will went into the kitchen to refill the chip bowl, he found his dad in civilian clothes, fixing himself a sandwich.

"Nice bunch of kids," Will's dad said. "But I've got to ask you something. Does that kid really *glow*?"

"Sometimes," Will answered, pouring chips into the bowl.

His dad shook his head. "Boy, they have really lowered the bar for heroes."

Will put the chip bag back into the cupboard. "Actually, Dad, he's a sidekick."

The Commander looked relieved. "Oh, well, that makes sense."

"Actually, Dad," Will said, "they all are."

The Commander looked surprised but also proud. "Good for you, son. A kid of your stature hanging out with a bunch of sidekicks? I mean, I never would have had the guts."

"There's nothing wrong with being a sidekick, Dad," Will said.

"No, no, of course not!" said the Commander. "I wasn't saying that—I love sidekicks. Used to have one myself. Saved my life once. Ol' what's-his-name . . ."

Will took a deep breath. "So you'd be okay if, you know . . . I was a sidekick?"

"Of course!" said the Commander. He peered over Will's shoulder. "Pass the mayo?"

"Good," said Will, "because I am."

"Am what?" asked the Commander.

"A sidekick," said Will.

"Who is?"

"Me. I'm a sidekick, okay? I washed out of power placement."

The Commander was stunned. In the living room, the rest of the sidekicks held their breath. They'd overheard the entire conversation.

"My son. A sidekick," the Commander said. He slammed his fist down. Everything on the counter bounced into the air.

"Boomer," the Commander said, shaking his head in disgust. "Couldn't make the big time, so now he thinks he can pass judgment on the real 'heroes' kids? It's a power trip, that's all it is. 'Sonic Boom'? Try 'Gym Teacher Man.'"

The Commander grabbed the phone.

"Dad, what are you doing?" Will asked.

"Calling the school," said his father.

"Dad, don't," Will said.

The Commander glanced down at his hand. He'd accidentally crushed the cordless phone.

"Dagnabbit," he said. He tossed the destroyed phone into the trash and yanked open a drawer full of spare cordless phones that he kept handy.

"Dad, it's not Coach Boomer," Will said. "It's me. I don't have any powers."

Will's father stared at him in disbelief. "But you will," he said. "You're just a late bloomer."

"Maybe, maybe not," Will said. "But you know what? I don't even care anymore, 'cause the fact is, I'm proud to be a sidekick."

Will grabbed the chip bowl and started back into the living room. "And by the way," he said, turning and staring his father straight in the eyes, "it's 'hero support.'"

Back in the living room, Will casually sat down.

"So I think we pretty much covered the undead," he said, setting the chip bowl on the table. "What's next?"

When no one said anything, Will glanced up. The others were staring at him in awe.

"What?" Will asked pointedly.

As Ethan opened his book and began reading a word problem out loud, Layla caught Will's eye and smiled at him proudly.

CHAPTER 5

Now that he'd told his dad, Will felt as if a huge weight had been lifted from his shoulders. The next day at school was the best one yet. Until lunchtime.

Will was walking into the lunchroom with his tray when something—or someone—tripped him right as he was passing Warren Peace. Everything on Will's tray ended up in Warren's lap.

"Sorry," Will said.

Warren stood up. "You will be," he said, glaring at Will.

"Warren, man, let's not do this," said Will. "I'm sorry my dad put your dad in jail, but—"

"No one talks about my dad!" Warren thundered. And then he ignited. One moment he was a regular kid—the next, a flaming human torch!

At a nearby table, Lash and Speed were loving it. "Oh, it is *so* on," Lash said.

Will grabbed a tray and held it up like a shield. Warren incinerated it with a fireball.

At the sidekicks' table, Will's friends were looking on in horror.

"Not promising," Magenta said dryly.

Will dropped the smoldering remains of the tray and ran for the fire alarm. *If I can only activate the sprinkler system*, he thought.

But Lash wasn't about to let that happen. His hand stretched across the room and grabbed Will's ankle, tripping him—for the second time.

Will rolled under a row of tables and crawled to the end. He looked up. Warren was standing on top of the table, fire coming out of every pore.

"Where're your sidekicks, Sidekick?" Warren asked.

"Right here!" Ethan cried, jumping forward.

Warren turned sharply, flames roaring. Ethan morphed into a puddle.

"Anyone else?" Warren asked the rest of Will's friends.

Will's fear turned to anger. "Leave them alone!" he shouted. He jumped to his feet . . . and lifted the entire table!

"I'm strong?" Will said in disbelief.

He hurled the table—and Warren with it—across the cafeteria and into the far wall.

"I'm superstrong!"

Will spun around and glared at Speed and Lash. "Now, who tripped me?" he demanded.

In a blur, Speed was gone. Looking scared, Lash raised his hands as if he was giving up . . . and then extended them to the ceiling, grabbed a light, and pulled himself up out of reach.

"Will!" shouted Zach. Will turned to find Warren charging at him.

Zach tossed Will a fire extinguisher. Will swung it across his body, clocking Warren in the face. Warren went down, hard.

Will's eyes opened wide in surprise. He didn't know his own strength.

"Hey! You okay?" he asked.

Warren looked up with a glint of fury in his eye. "Think I can't take a hit?" He burst into full flame and advanced on Will.

Will backed up, fiddling with the fire extinguisher. Finally he just ripped the top off. The explosion of foam showered Warren.

"Aaaarrrrgh!" Warren cried as the flames dancing over his skin died.

For a moment there was only silence; then the room erupted with applause. Will turned to find everyone cheering him. His friends looked relieved. Gwen flashed him that awesome smile.

Will smiled back. He was feeling pretty good . . . until the crowd parted and Principal Powers stepped through.

Uh-oh, Will thought.

That evening when Will got home, the first thing he did was rip the front door off its hinges.

Oops! He still wasn't used to his newfound strength, and he wasn't sure, but he felt as if he was getting stronger and stronger.

He stepped through the doorway and placed the door back in its frame, then turned to find both his parents waiting for him.

"So, Will," said his mom, "anything interesting happen at school today?"

Will couldn't keep the big grin off his face. "Well, as you may have noticed . . . *I got my powers!*"

In his enthusiasm, he picked his mother up with one arm.

"Yes, we know," his mom said in midair. She didn't seem as excited as he was. "The principal called."

Will gingerly set his mother down. "Okay, look," he said, "I know it sounds bad."

"You nearly destroyed the cafeteria!" his mom said, exasperated.

"But, Mom!" Will said. "I got my powers!"

"And do you know how to use them wisely? Apparently not!" she retorted.

Will looked at his dad for help, but his father had been glaring at him in stony silence. "Sanctum," his dad said. "Now."

Father and son rode the poles down into the sanctum. There the Commander sternly said, "William Theodore Stronghold . . ."

His face broke into a huge grin. He opened his arms. "Come here!"

"You're not mad?" Will wheezed as his father crushed him in a powerful bear hug.

"My boy's got superstrength! How could I be mad?" The Commander yanked Will into another massive hug.

He let go of his son and said, "Now, just in case your mother asks, tell her I read you the riot act and took away your game box."

"I don't have a game box," Will said.

His father handed him a wrapped present. "You do now!"

Meanwhile, in their secret lair, Royal Pain and Stitches were watching Will and the Commander thanks to the robot-eye spy cam.

"The boy has Stronghold's power," said Royal Pain. "It's almost poetic. . . ."

"We should crush them now," said Stitches, gleefully slamming his fist into his open palm. "We know he has the weapon—"

"Patience," said Royal Pain. "We've waited this long. When the time is right, we'll have our revenge."

"You know," said Stitches, suddenly thoughtful, "the time might pass a little quicker if we had a game box. . . ."

CHAPTER 6

The next morning, Will and the rest of the sidekicks were talking in the classroom before the first bell. They were excited, to say the least.

"Dude, you made sidekick history!" crowed Zach.

Will shrugged. "I don't know about that."

"Seriously," Ethan said. "From now on, people mess with us at their own peril."

Layla laid her hand on Will's arm. "You're breaking down barriers, Will," she said. "You're proving to everyone in this school that we're not 'heroes' or 'sidekicks,' we're just people. *Super* people."

Mr. Boy rushed in, looking flustered. "Seats, please!" he called. "Not you, Mr. Stronghold.

Gather your gear; you've been transferred to hero class."

Mr. Boy handed Will a new class schedule.

Will was shocked. "But what about . . ."

He looked at his friends. They were all smiling at him.

"We'll still see you on the bus," Ethan said.

"And we'll hang at lunch," said Zach.

Magenta tried her best to smile, but it still looked more like a grimace. "Right after you're finished dunking Ethan's head in the toilet," she said under her breath.

Will smiled back at them. He grabbed his backpack and turned to go, but stopped in the doorway. He turned and looked at Layla.

She smiled. "Just go already!"

Will turned again, squared his shoulders, and walked through the door.

According to his new schedule, he was supposed to be in Medulla's Mad Science Class. He walked down the hall and ducked into the lab. Medulla was in the middle of a lecture, his oversized brain pulsing.

"Rays!" he was saying. "From the silliness of the Shrink Ray to the devastation of the Death Ray. These are the very foundations of Mad Science. . . ."

Medulla noticed Will standing in the doorway. He seemed less than impressed. "Yes, they told me you were coming. Unfortunately, all the lab partners are taken. I suppose I'll have to pair you with my teaching assistant. Ms. Grayson, my apologies."

Sitting in the back of the room, smiling at Will, was Gwen. Will couldn't believe his luck.

After Medulla's lecture, the class broke up into their pairs and got to work on the experiment of the day. Leaning over a scarred lab table, Will frowned as he tried to fit high-tech parts together.

"Okay, how's that?" he asked Gwen, who was standing close beside him.

"Perfect," said Gwen. "If you're building a heat ray. But you're supposed to be building a freeze ray."

THE COMMANDER AND JETSTREAM MAKE
MORE THAN JUST A GREAT TEAM.

WILL AND HIS BEST FRIEND, LAYLA, HEAD
TO SKY HIGH ON THEIR FIRST DAY.

THE FRESHMEN HAVE TO DEMONSTRATE
THEIR SUPERPOWERS FOR CLASS PLACEMENT.

MR. BOY TEACHES THE SIDEKICK CLASSES.

THE COMMANDER SHOWS OFF SOME MEMENTOS FROM HIS GREATEST BATTLES.

NOW THAT WILL IS AT SKY HIGH, HIS DAD IS FINALLY SPENDING TIME WITH HIM.

POWERS OR NO POWERS, WILL IS DETERMINED
TO BE MORE THAN A SIDEKICK.

WARREN PEACE HAS A FIERY TEMPER
AND A STRONG DISLIKE FOR WILL.

ROYAL PAIN AND STITCHES MAKE A ROYAL
ENTRANCE AT THE HOMECOMING DANCE.

WITH ROYAL PAIN IN CONTROL, IT'S UP TO
THE SIDEKICKS TO SAVE THE SCHOOL.

LAYLA HAS BEEN HIDING HER PLANT
POWERS UP UNTIL NOW . . .

. . . AS THE MULTIPLE PENNYS QUICKLY FIND OUT.

"Oh, no," Will moaned. He glanced at Medulla, who was checking in with each team and evaluating their progress.

"Dreadful technique," Medulla was saying. "D. I'd give you an F, but that would only mean seeing you in summer school."

Will turned back to the jumble of parts in front of him, but the harder he tried, the less sense it made. Beside him, Gwen couldn't help laughing.

"And what have we here?" It was Medulla.

Will spun around, hiding the mess of parts from the teacher. "Mr. Medulla! Actually, I was having some trouble . . ."

Behind Will's back Gwen passed her hand over the scattered pieces, which instantly assembled themselves into an awesome tabletop ray gun.

Medulla peeked over Will's shoulder. "You're far too modest, Mr. Stronghold," he said.

Will turned in surprise as Medulla activated the gun. A cold blast shot out of it and froze a kid across the room.

Medulla eyed Gwen, suddenly suspicious. "Or perhaps not modest enough," he said.

"Ms. Grayson, in the future, please allow the students to succeed or fail on their own."

Will was still trying to understand what had happened. To Gwen he said, "But . . . you . . . how?"

Gwen shrugged. "I'm a technopath. I have control over technology."

"Wow," Will said. "All I can do is punch stuff."

Medulla walked off, shaking his head. "But he'll be the one on cereal boxes. Show me the justice in that. Ms. Fernandez!" he called across the room. "Kindly thaw out Mr. Hellman."

"That was amazing," Will said to Gwen.

"So's what you did in the cafeteria," said Gwen.

"Yeah, I'll be in good shape when they start handing out grades for wrecking school property."

Gwen laughed. "You know," she said, "I can totally help you with this science stuff."

"Yeah?" Will said. "You'd do that?"

"Mmm-hmm . . . ," Gwen said. She tucked her hair behind one ear. "I could be your private tutor."

Will liked the sound of that.

He was still hanging with Gwen at lunchtime. Carrying their trays, they walked into the lunchroom together.

"Hey, there's Penny!" said Gwen, heading right to her table. Will followed, feeling a little nervous.

Penny was sitting with two other upperclassmen.

"Will, this is Trevor and Jill," Gwen said.

Trevor nodded at Will. "That was some smackdown you gave Warren."

"Yeah," Jill agreed. "It was about time someone taught him a lesson."

Despite himself, Will felt his chest puff up a bit. "Oh, it's no big deal," he said modestly.

Just then he spotted his friends coming into the lunchroom with their trays.

"Guys, over here!" he called.

Looking uncertain, Layla, Zach, Ethan, and Magenta headed over. Just as they reached the table, Penny multiplied and filled every available seat.

"Sorry," she said brightly. "All full."

"Come on, guys," Layla said. "There's an empty table over here."

As the sidekicks moved off, Penny leaned toward Will. "A little advice, Will," she said. "We are not running a loser outreach program."

Trevor and Jill laughed, but Gwen shot Penny a disapproving look. As one of the Pennys launched into a story, Gwen said quietly to Will, "She can be a little harsh sometimes."

"They're not losers, you know," Will said.

"Of course they're not," Gwen said. "Just sidekicks. Will, you're a hero now. You're in a whole different league. It's just something to keep in mind."

But Will didn't feel right about what had happened. After lunch he found Layla at her locker.

"Hey, Layla," he said tentatively. "Listen, about lunch today . . ."

"What about it?" Layla asked, not exactly cold, but not her usual friendly self, either. She opened her locker. Inside was a huge flowering vine.

"You know, at the table," Will said. "Penny was being a total—"

"Please," Layla interrupted. "Not a big deal."

"I know, I just feel bad," said Will. "Let me make it up to you. How 'bout we hit the Paper Lantern tonight?"

"But you hate Chinese food," Layla said.

"But *you* don't," said Will.

Layla smiled. "Paper Lantern," she said. "Eight o'clock."

Will was about to say something else when from behind him he heard, "Hey, come on, guys! Quit it!"

He turned to find Speed and Lash stuffing Ethan into his locker.

Will walked over. "Okay, guys, let him go," he said.

Speed jerked his head at Lash. "You heard the man," he said.

Lash let go of Ethan and leaned against the next locker over. As Ethan was climbing out, Will noticed a green glow coming from the locker Lash was leaning against.

Will sighed. "And Zach, too," he said.

Lash rolled his eyes and opened the locker. Zach climbed out.

As Zach brushed himself off, he said, "Not so tough when my boy's around, are you?"

Speed glared at Will. "Oh. You think you're so bad, Stronghold?"

"I didn't say anything!" Will said calmly, trying to keep the conversation friendly.

Ethan crossed his arms. "Please," he said to Speed. "He can totally take you."

"You saw what happened to Warren," said Zach. "You want a piece of that?"

Speed poked Will in the shoulder. "Watch it, Stronghold, or that big mouth of yours is going to get you in trouble."

Will turned to Zach and Ethan. "Would you two stop it?" he pleaded.

"Tell you what," Speed said. "How 'bout we settle this in PE?"

"You're on!" Ethan said. "If Will beats you in Save the Citizen, you lay off the sidekicks for the rest of the year."

"And if Will loses," said Zach, "you can dunk Ethan's head in the toilet every day for a year."

"Yeah!" Ethan agreed. Then his eyes widened with the realization of what he had just agreed to. "Hey!"

"Deal!" Lash said. He and Speed turned and walked off, laughing.

Will looked at his friends in horror. "Are you guys crazy? No freshman has ever won Save the Citizen, and those guys are undefeated."

Layla came up behind them. "And you just got your powers!" she said.

Will gave her a look.

"Sorry," she said sheepishly. "Not helping."

"Will, you have no choice," Zach said gravely. "You can't let them dunk Ethan in the toilet. Not again."

CHAPTER
7

That afternoon the sidekick class was participating for the first time in Save the Citizen, a game designed to test their ability to use their powers creatively under pressure.

The gym had been transformed into something resembling a hockey rink, with Plexiglas panels in place around the floor to protect the spectators. Inside the Plexiglas ring were lampposts, mailboxes, and other things simulating objects on a city street. In the center of the arena was a set of huge mechanical jaws—the jaws of death.

Coach Boomer presided over the action from a tall referee's chair.

The first game was just coming to an end. The

kids not in that round were sitting in the bleachers, counting down with the clock. "Three, two, one!"

Bzzzz!

The scoreboard above the gym floor flashed GAME OVER as a mannequin was lowered into the jaws of death and chewed to bits.

Coach Boomer blew his whistle. "Ramirez, Hamilton, the citizen is dead, and it's all your fault," he called. "Speed. Lash. Your winning streak continues."

Speed and Lash celebrated with a high five as Ramirez and Hamilton slunk off the floor.

"Next round," called Coach Boomer. "Speed, Lash, you want to be heroes or villains?"

Speed grinned. "Villains," he said.

"No kidding," said Coach Boomer. "So, who do you want to beat next?"

Speed looked directly at Will. "We'll take little Stronghold and . . . let's see . . . how about . . ."

Speed scanned the students in the stands, then stopped. "Peace!"

Warren Peace! Will and Warren stared at each other in horror.

Above the floor, the scoreboard reset to three minutes on the clock. A new "hostage" was lowered from the ceiling toward the mechanical jaws.

Will and Warren stepped onto the battlefield.

"Hothead! Stronghold!" called out Coach Boomer. "You're the heroes; you got three minutes to get past Speed and Lash and save the citizen. Ready . . . set . . ."

Will glanced at Gwen in the stands. She nodded at him.

Warren growled, "Get your head in the game, loser!"

"BATTLE!" yelled the coach.

Lash stretched his arm out and grabbed a streetlight. Speed used Lash's elastic arm like the ropes of a wrestling ring, running into it and bouncing off. At super speed he rammed into Warren and Will, sending both flying.

"That's what I'm talking about!" Lash crowed as he let go of the streetlight and wrapped his arms tightly around Warren like a boa constrictor. Warren ignited, and Lash immediately let go, his hands on fire.

Warren launched a fireball at him, but Lash bent out of the way. The fireball flew across the arena and blew out part of the coach's chair.

"Hothead, watch it!" Coach Boomer yelled as he doused the fire with water from his sports bottle.

As the clock ticked down and the civilian got closer and closer to the jaws of death, Speed ran circles around Will. He was throwing superspeed punches that Will couldn't see coming, let alone dodge.

"That's right, Stronghold!" Speed cried. "Can't even lay a finger on me!"

"Maybe I don't have to," Will said. Summoning all his strength, Will smashed both fists into the floor. It was the same move his father had used against Royal Pain all those years ago. The shock wave knocked Warren off his feet and Speed into a mailbox. Lash crashed into a lamppost and crumpled to the floor.

Will grabbed Lash's stretched arms and tied them around the lamppost in an elaborate bow.

The students went wild. Even the coach chuckled behind his clipboard.

Will was looking proudly at the crowd when a fireball flew right by his ear. He spun around. Warren was launching fireball after fireball at Speed, but Speed was too fast to hit. He ran around Warren faster and faster, creating a vortex that sucked all the oxygen away. Suddenly, Warren's flames went out, and Warren dropped to his knees, gasping. He couldn't breathe!

Will reached into the vortex and grabbed Speed. Speed's legs spun in midair. Then Will put Speed down, aiming him right at the tied-up Lash.

"No, dude," Lash screamed. "Dude! *Dude!*"

Speed rammed him at full speed, taking out a piece of the lamppost and falling to the ground, momentarily stunned.

As the crowd erupted into cheers, Will glanced at the clock. They had only seconds before the citizen was munched. Quickly, Will turned, grabbed Warren, and launched him through the air at the citizen.

At the last possible moment, Warren shot a fireball at the rope holding the citizen, then grabbed her on the way by. He landed, rolled, then held up the citizen for the coach to see.

The buzzer sounded, ending the game.

"She's alive!" Coach Boomer roared. "HEROES WIN!"

Will looked around, amazed, as the crowd jumped to its feet, shouting and cheering. Will reached out a hand to help Warren up, but Warren only glared at Will, stood, and stalked off the floor.

He started over to the sidekicks, but the hero kids rushed onto the floor and mobbed him. Will looked back at the sidekicks apologetically as the heroes pulled him away.

CHAPTER 8

That night, Will and his dad came up from the secret sanctum.

"Son of a gun," the Commander said to Will, clapping him on the shoulder. "First you win Save the Citizen as a freshman, then you top your mom's high score on the pinball machine."

There was a burst of laughter from the kitchen. Sitting at the table with Will's mom was—to Will's surprise—Gwen.

The ladies turned, and Will's dad cleared his throat meaningfully.

"Oh, Dad," Will said. "This is Gwen Grayson. Gwen, this is—"

Gwen stood and held out her hand. "Commander, it is such an honor," she said with admiration. "I'm sorry to barge in like this."

"Not at all," the Commander said, shaking Gwen's hand.

"Hon, Gwen here is a technopath," said Will's mom. "She's offered to help Will with his science homework . . . and she's a *senior*."

Will's dad cocked an eyebrow at him. He was impressed.

Gwen smiled. "Will," she said, "I know we were going to work on that antigravity stuff tomorrow, but something came up. Any chance we could do it tonight?"

"Sure," Will said, lost in Gwen's stunning smile.

The Commander spoke up. "On one condition, Gwen," he said. "You join us for dinner."

"Oh, I couldn't intrude—"

"Come on, sure you can," Will urged.

"Okay, well . . . thanks!" she said, and then turned to Will. "Should we get started?"

Across town at the Paper Lantern, Layla was sitting alone at a table for two. The place was half empty. A waitress approached.

"I'll give him a few more minutes," Layla said.

The waitress shrugged and walked off. Layla glanced at a vase on the table that held a cheerful tulip. She stared at it, and the tulip slowly wilted.

At the Stronghold residence, Gwen, Will, and his parents had eaten dinner and were digging into bowls of ice cream.

"So I did have an ulterior motive in coming here tonight," Gwen was saying. "Will may have told you I'm on the Homecoming committee?"

"He most certainly did not," said the Commander.

"Well," Gwen continued, "I was wondering if you two would consider attending the Homecoming dance."

"We'd be happy to chaperone," said Jetstream.

Gwen shook her head. "We were hoping you'd be the guests of honor and receive the award for Heroes of the Year."

Mrs. and Mr. Stronghold looked at each other, flattered.

▼

At the Paper Lantern, an annoyed and sad Layla was the last customer in the place.

A busboy came to the table. "You still working on that?" he asked, gesturing at the plate of food she had hardly touched.

Layla looked up. It was Warren Peace!

"Hey," she said. "We go to school together."

Warren nodded. "You're Stronghold's friend."

"Yeah," Layla said with an apologetic shrug.

Warren picked up her plate. "You want me to heat that up for you?"

"You're not supposed to use your powers outside of school," Layla said.

"I was just going to stick it in the microwave," said Warren, giving her a teasing smirk.

Layla smiled. "I was supposed to be meeting Will here, but . . ."

She trailed off uncomfortably, then asked, "Hey, do you want to sit down?"

Warren glanced around the empty restaurant. "I think I can spare a minute."

As he sat, he smiled and lit the candle on the table with his finger.

Back at the Stronghold residence, Will and Gwen were sitting on the couch together, thumbing through an old Sky High yearbook. The Commander and Jetstream stood behind the couch, pointing things out.

"Look, hon," said the Commander. "There's what's-his-name, the kid with the gravity."

"Lance, I think," said Jetstream. "Lance something. And there's Boomer."

Will did a double take. "He had a mullet?"

They all laughed as Will turned the page.

"Whoa, remember her?" the Commander said, pointing out an intense, nerdy-looking girl with flat hair, glasses, and gleaming braces.

"Oh, yeah," Jetstream said. "Sue Tenney. She disappeared right before graduation."

"Why is that?" Gwen asked.

"No one ever really knew," said Jetstream. "Some say she was caught recruiting villains at the school."

Meanwhile, Layla was talking up a storm as she munched on a fortune cookie.

"And there was this time in first grade," she was saying. "You know how you grow lima beans in school? Well, Will couldn't figure out why mine was growing so fast. It was totally driving him crazy. Then finally I told him about my powers, and we've been best friends ever since."

"And falling for him," said Warren. "Was that before or after the lima beans?"

"What?" Layla cried. "That's insane!"

Warren gave her a disbelieving stare.

"Before," Layla admitted with a sigh. "But he doesn't know. I was going to ask him to Homecoming, but there are two problems. He likes someone else, and she's perfect."

"You know what I think?" asked Warren, suddenly serious. "To let true love remain unspoken is the quickest route to a heavy heart."

Layla was blown away.

"Wow," she said. "That's . . . that is really deep. It sounds like you're talking from personal experience."

"Not so much," he said. Then he held up the fortune from her fortune cookie. And they both started to laugh.

Will was walking Gwen home. They had just turned up the sidewalk to Gwen's house.

"You really didn't have to walk me home," Gwen said.

"I did if I wanted any time alone with you," said Will. "And just so you know, I don't usually hang out all night with my mom and dad."

They stepped onto Gwen's front porch.

"Your parents are great, Will," said Gwen. "I'm glad they're coming to Homecoming. Now if only I could find someone to go with . . ."

"Wait," said Will. "You mean you don't have a date for Homecoming?"

Gwen shrugged. "I got some offers, but I turned

them down. I've been waiting for the right guy. . . ."

Gwen smiled as Will, dumbfounded, pointed to himself.

"Me?" he asked.

"*You*, Will."

Just as they leaned in to kiss, the front door flew open. Gwen pulled away as her dad stepped into the doorway. Mr. Grayson was a serious-looking man with a pipe and a cardigan sweater.

"Oh! Hi, Daddy," Gwen said innocently.

Mr. Grayson eyed Will distrustfully. "You're not that boy with four arms, are you?" he asked.

"No, sir," Will said. "Just two."

"Well, keep them to yourself," Mr. Grayson said.

"Dad!" Gwen cried, embarrassed. Quickly she leaned into Will and gave him a kiss on the cheek, then hurried inside. The door closed behind her.

Will took a step back, turned, and leapt off the porch onto a lamppost. He giddily swung around it . . . and accidentally yanked it down.

Will looked around and quickly replaced

the post. Then he headed home with a spring in his step.

In their secret lair, Royal Pain and Stitches were sitting in front of the viewscreen, scrutinizing the Commander's secret sanctum.

"Homecoming," Royal Pain mused. "The greatest collection of superteens ever gathered to dance under one roof. That is when we shall have our revenge. There's only one thing we're missing."

Royal Pain smiled wickedly behind his mask as he zoomed in on the Pacifier.

CHAPTER 9

The next morning, at the bus stop, Layla and Will met up. Will was beaming.

"You're never going to guess what happened to me last night!" Will said.

Layla held out her hand to Will. She was holding a fortune cookie.

"Oh, thanks," Will said, picking it up and taking a bite. "I love these things. Okay, so last night—"

Suddenly Will remembered. "Layla, I totally spaced! You must want to kill me!"

Layla laughed. "Actually, just the opposite," she said. "I have to tell you something."

"Yeah?" Will asked.

"But you first," Layla said. "What's up?"

"It's about Homecoming—"

"Really?" Layla said. "Me too."

"I'm going with Gwen Grayson!" Will said. "Can you believe it? Me, a freshman, going to Homecoming with the most amazing girl at Sky High!"

The smile on Layla's face froze. After her talk with Warren, she had finally decided to tell Will how she felt. Instead, she now had to call on every ounce of strength she had and force out, "That's awesome!"

The bus pulled up, and they boarded. It wasn't until they were in the air that Will remembered about Layla.

"Oh, I almost forgot!" Will said. "What's your Homecoming news?"

Layla thought for a second, then said, "I'm going, too."

"Really?" Will asked. "Cool! Who with?"

"Who with?" Layla asked, stalling.

"Yeah, who asked you?"

"Oh, who asked me," Layla said. "Um . . . Warren Peace."

Will laughed. "Yeah, Warren Peace! Come on, really, who asked you? Zach? Ethan?"

Layla found Will's amusement less than amusing. "I told you," she said matter-of-factly.

"Warren Peace!" he said, no longer smiling about it. "You can't be serious."

Layla nodded nonchalantly. Apparently she'd touched a nerve.

"Layla, the guy's a psycho and like my biggest enemy in the school!" Will said. "How could you go with him? When did you even start hanging out with him?"

Layla looked Will right in the eye. "Last night. Eight o'clock. Paper Lantern," she said flatly.

At lunch, Warren was sitting at his usual table with his usual company—no one—when Layla swooped down next to him.

"Hi, Warren!" she said with a big smile.

Warren barely looked at her. "Did I do or say anything last night to make you think this is okay?"

Layla tilted back her head and laughed as if that was the funniest thing she'd ever heard. "But seriously," she said, suddenly getting serious, "you're not going to believe what happened. I was about to ask Will to Homecoming, but wouldn't you know it, I told him I was going with you instead!"

Warren stared at Layla as if she'd lost her mind. "I don't remember that being the plan," he finally said.

Just then Magenta plopped down next to Layla. "Hey, Layla. Did you do that history homework?"

Then Ethan slid into a seat with his tray. He was excited. "Are we eating at Warren's table now?" he asked.

"Whoa, whoa . . . ," Warren said, not exactly comfortable with his new popularity.

Zach swaggered up. "This guy bothering you, Layla?" he asked.

"Try the other way around," Warren grumbled. "Does anyone else need a date to Homecoming?"

Ethan raised his hand.

Layla burst out with an extremely shrill laugh.

"Oh, Warren! You really are *so* crazy!"

Will passed their table, looking concerned. He was with Gwen.

As soon as Will had gone, Layla whispered, "Warren, I promise, I'll make it as painless as possible."

Warren suddenly understood. "So you're not doing this because you like me or anything," he said. "You're just doing this to get to Stronghold."

Layla's shoulders dropped. "Yes," she admitted.

Warren smiled maliciously. "Then I'm in." He stood up to go. "But I am *not* renting a tux."

That night, Will and Gwen were studying in his bedroom. Will was blindfolded, and the parts for a shrink ray were spread out around him. He reached for one.

"Is this the trigger?" he asked.

"No," said Gwen, "that's the fusion device."

"Shoot," Will said. He reached out again. "Okay, what's this?"

"That's me," Gwen said.

Will blushed and took off his blindfold. He and

Gwen stared into each other's eyes. Will leaned in to kiss her, but at the same moment, Gwen's cell phone rang.

"Hello?" Gwen said, answering it. "What? I can't— Penny, I can't understand you when you're all talking at once. . . . Better . . . What? Oh, no . . . Okay, hold on."

"What is it?" Will asked.

"There's a problem with the decorations for Homecoming," Gwen said. She was obviously worried. The dance was the next night. "Penny forgot to order the fog machine, and I might have to build one myself. You think the committee can stop by here?"

"Uh, I don't know," Will said. "My parents are out on a distress call. They won't be home till late. I'm not really supposed to—"

"Hey, it's cool," said Gwen. She stood up to go.

"You know," Will said reluctantly, "if it's just a few people. . . ."

Thirty minutes later, Will's house was party

zone central. Music was blaring, and the house was packed with kids. A disco ball had been hung from the ceiling of the living room, and a kid with laser eyes was staring at it, sending colored light dancing around the room.

Will walked through the party, totally stressed. Big Larry, the kid who could turn to stone, sat down on one end of the couch, sending a kid sitting at the other end flying into the ceiling. Penny had multiplied, and each of her was talking up a different guy.

A couple of girls looked on with irritation. "Every party she does this," one of them said. "And of course, it's only the cute guys."

A spider kid climbed down the wall, grabbed a slice of pizza, and climbed back up.

"Gary!" Will called after him. "You're getting cheese all over the ceiling!"

Putting a coaster under a wet soda sitting on top of a speaker, he saw two kids dragging a tub filled with ice across the floor.

"*Guys!*" Will said, exasperated. He easily lifted the tub with one hand and slid a towel underneath it with the other.

In the kitchen Speed was raiding the refrigerator at high speed. Finally Will spotted Gwen and made a beeline for her.

"I thought you said the homecoming committee was coming over!" Will said.

"This is the homecoming committee," said Gwen innocently.

Will gave her a skeptical look.

"Okay, so a few extra people showed up," Gwen said. "But you're popular, Will. That's what happens."

"Gwen," said Will, "every kid in hero class is here! How am I ever going to get this place cleaned up in time?"

Speed had followed Will out of the kitchen. "I'll do the cleanup," he said. "It'll take me two minutes, tops."

As Will opened his mouth to argue, Gwen grabbed his hand and pulled him into the den. She shut the door, and the sounds of the party grew distant. They were alone.

"Okay," Gwen said, "what's on your mind?"

"Nothing," Will said. Then reluctantly he said, "Well . . . my friends."

"What about 'em?" Gwen asked. "They're all here. . . . Oh. You mean the sidekicks."

Will picked up the phone. "Maybe I should just call Zach and Layla."

Gwen gently took the phone from Will. "You're a sweet guy, Will," she said. "But honestly, do you think they'd have fun? With this crowd?"

"I think they'd probably be okay—"

"Trust me," said Gwen. "They'd be miserable. C'mere."

Gwen was leaning in close for a kiss when the door suddenly opened and the sounds of the party blasted into the room.

"Hey!" Gwen said.

It was Speed. "Sorry, sorry," he said. "Just looking for a bucket."

He backed out and closed the door. Gwen ran her fingers through Will's hair. "Isn't there anywhere else we can go?" she asked.

Will smiled. Moments later, he was showing her around the secret sanctum. Gwen was awestruck.

"This is incredible," she said.

"Yeah, well," Will said, proud, "when you spend your life kicking butt and taking names, I guess you make a lot of memories."

Gwen took Will's hand. "Why don't we make a few of our own?"

As she kissed Will, a blur of speed swept through the room, unnoticed.

Later, Will and Gwen emerged from the sanctum, laughing.

"Will," said Gwen, giving him her biggest smile, "could you go get me a diet caffeine-free orange soda?"

"For you?" Will said. "Anything."

As Will left for the kitchen, Gwen turned to the door, suddenly deadly serious.

It was Layla.

Walking home, she'd heard all the noise coming from Will's house, and she had come in to investigate. Now she was surrounded by a sea of Pennys.

"Who invited the sidekick?" one of the Pennys asked.

"Yeah, what's *she* doing here?" asked another.

"Leaving," Gwen said.

"Where's Will?" Layla asked.

"Honestly? Avoiding you," said Gwen.

Layla looked confused. Gwen said, "Look, he knows you have a crush on him—"

"He does?" asked Layla, mortified.

"Everyone does," Gwen assured her sweetly. "But Will's too nice a guy to tell you he's not interested. Not that you can take a hint. I mean, hello? He's going to Homecoming with *me*. He threw a party and didn't invite *you*."

Layla ran for the front door in tears just as Will came out of the kitchen with Gwen's soda.

"Layla?" Will called.

"Have fun with Gwen," Layla said to him. "You deserve each other."

Then she hurried out the door. Will walked back to Gwen, who was chatting with the Pennys.

"Oh, thanks, Will," Gwen said, taking the soda from him.

"What did you say to Layla?" Will demanded.

"Nothing," said Gwen. "I just told her the truth. You're a hero. She's a sidekick. She's holding you back."

"How could you—" Will said, choking back his anger. "Layla's been my best friend since first grade."

"Well, you've got new friends now," said Gwen. "And I think you've got to figure out if you want to hang with us or with those losers."

She smiled. To her, it was no contest.

Will looked around. His house was full of strangers.

"Forget it," he said. "Find yourself a new date, Gwen."

Gwen couldn't believe what she was hearing. "You're dumping me?" she asked incredulously. "*Whoa*. Let's get something straight. *You* do not dump *me*. Not the night before the dance."

"Sorry, Gwen, too late. I just did." Will turned his back on her. "Everyone out!" he yelled. "Party's over!"

"Don't stop on our account."

Standing by the back door was Will's father. His mother was right behind him.

"Your father and I go to Europe for two hours and you throw a party?" Jetstream asked.

The Commander scanned the room. "We get a distress call that turns out to be a false alarm. Now, was it a *real* false alarm, or just a way to get us out of the house?"

"Dad, I did not plan this," Will said.

Jetstream wasn't buying it. "Oh, no? Then who did?" she asked.

The room was dead silent.

"I see," said the Commander. "I'm going to count to three, and I want everyone out of this house. *One!*"

It didn't take more than that. A moment later, the house was empty.

The Commander looked at his son. "Will, I'm only going to ask you once—"

"Dad, I swear I didn't plan this."

The Commander was suddenly all smiles. "Good enough for me!"

Jetstream shook her head. "Well, I've got half

a mind not to let you go to Homecoming."

"Fine with me," Will said. "I'm not going anyway."

"*Whoa, whoa, whoa!*" said the Commander. "Your mom said *half* a mind. You have to go to Homecoming. We all do."

But Jetstream was staring at her son. She could tell something was wrong.

"What happened, Will?" she asked.

"I don't want to talk about it," Will said, really not wanting to talk about it.

The Commander wasn't giving up. "We promised Gwen we'd be at that dance. And when a Stronghold makes a promise, the promise is kept."

"I promise you, Dad," said Will coolly, "I am not going."

CHAPTER 10

Up in his room, Will was trying to call Layla. He kept getting the answering machine.

"Come on, Layla, pick up. Pick up!" Will said. He sighed. "Okay, don't pick up. I'm going to the Paper Lantern. If you get this message, please meet me there."

Will hung up. Like father like son, he crushed the phone in the process.

An hour and a half later, Will was sitting alone in a booth at the Paper Lantern. He was on his cell phone. "Okay, Layla, just in case you didn't get my earlier messages, I'm at the Paper—"

There was a beep and an automated message: "Memory full."

Will scowled and hung up. Warren walked

over. "What are you doing here?" he asked.

"Looking for Layla," Will said. "Do you know where she is?"

"Why should I know?" Warren asked.

"Uh . . . because you're dating her?"

"Oh, yeah. Right," said Warren, enjoying Will's pain.

"Look, do me a favor," said Will. "Make sure she has a great time at Homecoming. She deserves it."

"Well, she's not going to have a great time with me," Warren said.

"Why not?" Will asked.

"Because she was only going with me to make you jealous."

"Why would she want to make me . . . Oh."

The next evening was the Homecoming Dance. The gym had been decorated with balloons and banners. A disco ball flicked shards of light around the darkened room. Students, teachers, and parents danced to the music.

In one corner, Zach grooved quietly by himself. He glanced nervously at Magenta, who was standing nearby and looking irritated, as usual.

Screwing up his courage, Zach said, "You want to dance?"

"No," Magenta said.

"Me neither," he said, going back to quietly grooving.

Layla came in. For the occasion she'd put up her hair and worn makeup, but nothing could hide the sad expression on her face.

She walked over to the refreshments table, where Mr. Boy was ladling punch out of a large crystal bowl.

"Hey, Layla, you look like you can use a drink," he said. He offered her a cup. "Don't worry. The bubbles come from ginger ale."

"No, thanks," Layla said.

Ethan walked up and took the cup of punch. He nudged Layla to look over her shoulder. Warren had just walked through the door— looking dashing in black formal attire.

"I thought you weren't going to rent a tux,"

Layla said, shocked—and pleasantly surprised.

"It's my dad's," said Warren. "He doesn't have much use for it in solitary."

Layla stared at him for a moment, and then he gave her a just-kidding smile.

"So Will came by the restaurant yesterday. I'm pretty sure he knows you just asked me to the dance to make him jealous."

"How does he know that?" Layla asked.

Warren shrugged. "I told him."

Layla frowned. "Well, I don't care what Will thinks anymore. So I guess you can go do whatever you want now."

"Okay," Warren said, taking her hand and leading her to the dance floor.

For the first time that evening, Layla smiled.

At the Stronghold residence, Will was busy feeling sorry for himself. He sat in the secret sanctum, staring at his empty section of trophy wall. He picked up his parents' yearbook and thumbed through it until he found his dad's senior-year picture. The list of accomplishments below it was long: Student Body President; Save the Citizen, undefeated; Best Smile. The list went on.

Will sighed and started to close the book, but something caught his eye: a photo at the bottom of the page. It was Sue Tenney, the nerdy-looking girl his parents had talked about.

Will looked more closely. Sue Tenney somehow seemed familiar. The hair was drastically different, and Sue wore glasses and had braces . . . but there was a definite resemblance between this Sue Tenney and—Gwen!

"That's weird," Will said.

Below the photo, the only one activity listed was Science Club. Will flipped through the pages until he found a science club photo, in which Sue was posing with a handheld cannon. A handheld cannon that looked a whole lot like—

Fear shot through Will. He dropped the yearbook and turned back to the trophy wall. Sure enough, the Pacifier was gone!

"Oh, no," Will groaned. There was only one

possible explanation. Sue Tenney had been Royal Pain. Gwen was her daughter. Now Gwen was out to avenge her mother's death. Somehow, once Will had let her into the secret sanctum, she had managed to get the Pacifier out.

He had to get to Sky High!

But how? Then Will remembered the card that Ron the bus driver had given him on the first day of school, which seemed so long ago now.

Will whipped out the card and picked up the phone.

At Sky High, the Commander and Jetstream had just entered the gym. The Commander looked around with a frown.

"Tonight was supposed to be the unveiling of the Stronghold Three. It's just not the same without Will."

Jetstream nodded. "Maybe we should fly home."

The Commander was nodding as they were caught in the glare of a spotlight.

"Welcome, Commander and Jetstream!" boomed Principal Powers's voice over the PA.

Everyone in the room turned and applauded. It was too late to leave. The Commander and Jetstream put on big fake smiles and walked into the gym.

"Good evening!" Principal Powers continued. "First, a quick announcement. The owner of a blue cold-fusion-powered jet pack, you left your lights on."

Mr. Medulla sheepishly hustled out of the room, muttering.

"And now," said Principal Powers, "please help me welcome the head of the homecoming committee, the girl who made this all possible— Gwen Grayson!"

Gwen stepped onto the stage, holding a golden trophy. From the side of the room, Gwen's father watched proudly.

"Thanks, Principal Powers," Gwen said. "And a very special thanks goes to our guests of honor and the recipients of the first ever Hero of the Year Award, the Commander and Jetstream!"

Everyone in the auditorium applauded again.

"And to mark this occasion," Gwen continued, "we've planned a special tribute to the most powerful superbeing to ever walk the halls of Sky High—*me!*"

As everyone in the room looked on in stunned silence, nanobots crept over Gwen's entire body like an army of robotic bugs, covering her in a suit of armor. Gwen laughed, and her voice was now harsh and metallic. She now looked and sounded just like Royal Pain!

On the side of the room, Gwen's "father" had put on a jester's hat. It was Stitches! He jumped onto the stage with Gwen, joined by Speed, Penny, and Lash.

The Commander was thunderstruck. "Royal Pain is a . . . girl?"

"Yes, I'm a girl, you idiot!" Royal Pain's metallic voice thundered. "How I ever lost to a fool like you, I will never know."

"You can't be Royal Pain," Jetstream said. "Nothing survived that explosion."

"This did!" crowed Stitches. He reached

behind the podium and whipped out the fully repaired Pacifier.

Stitches handed the weapon to Royal Pain. She laughed again, her electronic voice merciless. "Now prepare to be pacified!"

The Commander stepped forward, unafraid. "You think you can kill me with that little toy gun of yours?" he asked.

"My dear Commander," said Royal Pain, "who said anything about killing you?"

With a *zap!* Royal Pain fired the Pacifier, sending a crackling blast of energy into the Commander's chest. In an instant, the Commander had disappeared and his uniform had fallen to the floor.

The heap of clothes began to squirm. Horrified, Jetstream reached into the clothes and pulled out a baby.

Everyone in the room gasped. Jetstream's expression went from shocked to enraged. She handed the baby Commander to Principal Powers and launched herself at Royal Pain.

"Why, you—" Jetstream called.

Royal Pain zapped her with the Pacifier, and Jetstream turned into a baby in mid flight.

"Bwaaah!" she cried as she plummeted through the air.

Mr. Boy sprang into action, catching her before she could hit the ground.

"Oh, yeah!" Mr. Boy cried. "Back in the game!"

But a moment later, he, too, was blasted by the Pacifier.

Medulla came running back into the gym. "What'd I miss?" he asked.

Zap! Instantly, he was morphed into a baby.

As Royal Pain blasted hero after hero, student after student, Penny, Speed, and Lash raced around the room, locking door after door. Stitches cackled like a crazed hyena. No one would escape Royal Pain's vengeance!

Behind the refreshments table, the sidekicks huddled in fear. Warren stepped past them, his fists igniting into flame.

"Hothead!" called Coach Boomer as he ran past. "Find an exit! Get out as many people as you can!"

"But I can—" Warren began to protest.

"Just do it!" the coach shouted before he, too, was turned into a baby.

Warren turned and shot a fireball at a big air vent, blasting away the grate.

"Let's go!" he called to the sidekicks.

One after the other, they dove through the vent, into the air duct. They crawled in a line for a few moments in silence. It was pitch-black.

Finally Magenta said, "Where the heck are— *ow!*"

"Watch your head," said Zach.

Ethan called out, "Warren, how about a torch?"

"Only if you want to get barbecued," Warren growled.

The next moment, a light green glow filled the duct. It was Zach!

As they followed Zach, Magenta began to sing softly, "Then all the reindeer loved him . . ."

CHAPTER 11

Will had reached Sky High, thanks to Ron Wilson, bus driver. He was racing down the hall when he noticed a green glow coming from an air vent. He paused as the grate popped out, and Warren and the sidekicks climbed out one by one.

"Guys, you're never going to believe this," Will began to explain breathlessly. "Gwen—"

"—is Royal Pain," Layla said.

"Yeah," said Will. "And—"

"She stole the Pacifier," said Warren.

"Yeah!" Will said.

"And then she turned everyone into babies," said Zach. "Including your parents!"

Will's eyes opened wide. "Okay, that I didn't know."

"What're we going to do, Will?" Ethan asked, near panic.

"We're going to stop her," Will said. "All of us."

"All of who?" asked Magenta. "You and Warren? The rest of us are just a bunch of sidekicks."

"It's not what you're called," Will said. "It's what you do. Having powers doesn't make you a hero. Sometimes it just makes you a jerk."

Will turned to Layla. "In case my Homecoming date ends up killing me, there's something I want you to know."

He pulled Layla to him and kissed her.

"*Aw*, isn't that sweet?"

The sidekicks whirled around to find Penny, Lash, and Speed blocking the hallway.

Will shook his head. "Why doesn't this surprise me?"

Warren and the sidekicks stepped in front of Will.

"Will, go take care of Gwen," Warren said, taking charge. "We'll handle these clowns."

Will nodded, then took a shortcut by smashing right through a wall.

Battle erupted in the hallway. Zach and Magenta ducked back into the air vent as Speed zoomed by, smashing into Warren and sending him skidding down the corridor.

Penny cartwheeled down the hall at Layla, multiplying as she went. Layla backed up warily.

Lash stretched out an arm to grab Ethan and yanked him in the other direction. He pinned Ethan to the wall with one outstretched arm and sent his fist flying toward Ethan's face with the other. At the last moment, Ethan morphed into a puddle and slipped out of Lash's grip.

Wham! Lash's fist slammed into the wall.

As Ethan sloshed under the door to the men's room, Lash shouted, "Come back and fight!"

He followed Ethan into the men's room and smacked open stall after stall. Each was empty.

"Can't hide forever, sidekick!"

Finally Lash opened the last stall. The toilet lid was down. Lash grinned as he stepped into the stall and lifted the lid. Behind him,

Ethan re-formed. He kicked Lash from behind, and Lash's head ended up in the toilet bowl. Ethan flushed, and Lash's neck stretched as his head disappeared.

"Sucks for you," Ethan said. He dashed out of the men's room and saw Warren and Speed headed right for him. Warren was launching fireballs, but Speed was just too fast and dodged each one—until he stepped into a strange, slick puddle and lost his footing. Warren blasted Speed into a locker and welded the door shut.

"Nice work," Warren said as the puddle transformed into Ethan once more.

In the meantime, the Pennys had backed Layla into the cafeteria.

"Two, four, six, eight, who will we eliminate?" the Pennys chanted. "Layla, Layla, *noooooo* Layla!"

Layla furiously ducked a barrage of kicks and punches from all around her.

"Come on, sidekick," one of the Pennys said,

taunting Layla. "Aren't you going to fight back?"

Layla gasped out an answer as she bobbed and weaved. "I don't believe . . . *umph* . . . in using my powers . . . *uhh* . . . for violence."

"Really?" said another Penny. In sequence, one Penny after the other said: "I—live—for—it!"

Finally one of Penny's fists connected with Layla's jaw. Layla's head snapped to the side. When she turned back, there was a new look in her eye.

"Big mistake," she said.

Outside the cafeteria, the school's garden suddenly came to life. As Layla concentrated, vines and tendrils burst through the windows and wrapped around the ankles, waists, and wrists of the Pennys, lifting them until they were dangling from the ceiling.

"But . . . I thought you were a sidekick," one of the Pennys said in confusion.

"I *am* a sidekick," said Layla proudly. She turned to go.

"Wait!" Penny pleaded. "Don't leave us here to die."

"Relax," Layla said. "It's just *Lycopersicon esculentum*. You'll be fine."

"No," Penny said. "Royal Pain put a scrambler on the antigravity generator!"

Another of the Pennys chimed in. "The whole school's going to fall out of the sky!"

In the gym, all the students and faculty had been pacified. Royal Pain and Stitches had packed each of the new babies into a car seat and were transporting them on a conveyor belt to the parking lot.

Royal Pain was walking back and forth, carrying the baby Commander, while Stitches loaded the rest of the babies into one of the school buses.

"I take you back, my dear Commander, to your senior year at Sky High. A time before anyone knew what a technopath was. So a brilliant but misunderstood girl named Sue Tenney was written off as a science geek and stuck in sidekick class.

"She hatched a plan—so daring, so visionary—

to start her very own supervillain academy and raise a generation of heroes from scratch as villains. But first she had to destroy the institution that dared to spurn her genius! And now, so many years later, that plan is complete.

"My only regret? That this may be the finest evil villain speech ever given, and you have no idea what I'm saying."

"But I do."

Royal Pain spun around to find Will standing between her and the school.

"I'm sorry my father killed your mother," Will said. "But turning a gym full of innocent heroes into babies won't change that fact."

"That 'fact' is a fiction," Royal Pain said, chuckling smugly. Stitches ran over, and she handed him the baby Commander.

"When the Pacifier exploded," Royal Pain continued, "I wasn't destroyed but returned to infancy. Stitches raised me as his own—"

"Daddy's little girl!" Stitches cackled proudly.

"*I told you never to call me that!*" Royal Pain screamed. She regained her composure and turned back to Will. "That's right. I'm not Sue's daughter. I *am* Sue."

Will was stunned.

"You mean . . . I made out with an old lady?"

Warren and Layla had assembled the rest of the sidekicks in the hallway to deal with the scrambler Royal Pain had put on the antigravity generator. They were looking at a blueprint of the school that Zach had grabbed from the office.

Layla pointed to the map. "Okay, here's the generator room—"

Magenta was shaking her head. "But Royal Pain sealed off every route to it."

Ethan pointed to something else. "What about this conduit?" he asked.

"Yeah, right," said Warren. "You'd have to be like a rat to fit in there."

Everyone looked at Magenta. For once, she smiled, and in seconds, a purple guinea pig was scurrying down a tiny conduit.

"Go about ten feet," Ethan called down the

shaft. "There should be an opening on your right."

The guinea pig turned the corner.

"Find the access panel," Ethan said. "It leads right to the generator."

Magenta pushed open a panel with her guinea pig nose. Right in front of her was the scrambler. It was covered in a tangle of red wires.

"Okay!" Ethan shouted. "Now all you need to do is cut the red wire!"

Irritated, the guinea pig had no choice but to start nibbling at the wires.

▼

Will and Royal Pain were locked in hand-to-hand combat. Thanks to her techno-armor, Royal Pain was just as strong as Will.

Gaining an advantage, Will picked up Royal Pain and sent her crashing headfirst down the refreshments table. She smashed into the punch bowl, shattering it into millions of pieces of glass.

Royal Pain sprang to her feet and grabbed the podium off the stage. She swung it at Will.

Will ducked. He grabbed Royal Pain around the waist and hurled her at the ceiling. She smashed into the disco ball and hung helpless for a moment.

She did a double kick, shattering the ball. She fell to the floor in a shower of broken mirror.

She lunged at Will again. He parried, but Royal Pain knocked the wind out of him with a powerful punch to the stomach. Will went down.

Royal Pain loomed over him, cocking her fist back for the finishing blow. Will grabbed her ankle and pulled her foot out from under her.

Just then Layla and Warren ran into the gym. "Will!" Layla called.

As Will glanced up, Royal Pain fingered some buttons on her gauntlet, sending an energy blast into Will's chest. Will flew back, smashing through the gym window and over the edge of Sky High.

"*No!*" Layla screamed.

Royal Pain climbed to her feet.

"There goes your last chance of stopping me," she said, gloating.

"We'll see about that!" Layla yelled. But Warren grabbed her before she could charge at Royal Pain.

A figure appeared behind Royal Pain. Layla couldn't believe it. It was Will! And he was flying!

Layla smiled. Royal Pain turned to see what she was looking at.

"Mom always hoped I'd be a flier," Will said, smashing into Royal Pain like a cannonball. Her face mask shattered. Royal Pain flew through the air and crashed into a far wall. She collapsed in a defeated heap.

Warren let Layla go. She ran across the gym to Will. He turned and caught her as she jumped into his arms. Neither of them noticed Gwen grasping for her gauntlet—and one final button.

Sky High suddenly lurched.

Will, Layla, and Warren screamed. The whole school plummeted toward the ground.

Will took off and flew through the window to the bottom of the school. Setting his shoulder against the platform, he flew up with all the force he could muster. But it wasn't enough. All he could do was slow Sky High's fall as Magenta continued to chew through the wires.

Will glanced down. Sky High was falling right

over a town! He strained with all his might as the ground rushed up at him. And then—

Will slowly opened his eyes. Sky High had stopped. Magenta had managed to deactivate the scrambler. Sky High's antigravity generator had kicked in about ten feet above the roof of a house.

The owners of the house stood outside and looked up at Will and the school in awe.

"I know Josie Stronghold said this house was close to a good school," the wife said, "but this is ridiculous."

CHAPTER 12

Will, Warren, and the sidekicks stood beside Royal Pain's school bus full of wailing babies. Ron the bus driver had tied up Stitches off to the side.

"Now what?" Layla asked.

"Beats me," said Will. "I'm superstrong and I can fly, but I'm no genius."

"Perhaps I can be of assistance."

It was baby Medulla, who looked just like any baby except for his huge pulsing brain.

"It should only take me a couple of hours to reconfigure the Pacifier," Medulla said in his eloquent but still babyish voice. "Mr. Peace, if you would please carry me to the Mad Science Lab . . ."

"Uh, sure," said Warren, a little weirded out.

"And, Mr. Peace?"

"Yeah?"

"Regrettably, I have made boom-boom."

They all looked at each other and wrinkled their noses.

A couple of hours later, crackling flashes of light were coming from the Mad Science Lab. Restored students and faculty were stumbling out, wrapped in blankets.

Principal Powers was one of the first ones restored. "People, if you've already been depacified, please grab a baby and report to the Mad Science Lab."

Will was talking with the Commander and Jetstream in the hallway.

"Mom, Dad, I'm so sorry," he said. "This was all my fault."

"Oh, honey," said his mom, "you can't blame yourself."

The Commander agreed. "How were you supposed to know your girlfriend was a psychopath?"

"That's not it," Will said, trying to find the right

words. "You gave me one rule, and I broke it."

A little confused, the Commander and Jetstream stared at Will. They weren't following him.

"I took her into the sanctum, Dad," Will explained. "That's how she got the Pacifier. The party was just a trap."

Ashamed, Will looked down at his feet. He was surprised when he felt his dad's hand on his shoulder.

"And so was this homecoming, Will," the Commander said. "We all fell into Royal Pain's trap. But you defeated her. You saved Sky High and everyone in it."

Will couldn't help smiling. "But," he pointed out, "I didn't do it myself."

Will looked over to where Warren, the sidekicks, and Ron Wilson, bus driver, were standing together and laughing as they talked about what they'd each done that evening.

Just then Mr. Boy approached with the Hero of the Year Award.

"Uh, Steve?" Mr. Boy said to the Commander.

"Even though it appears that Gwen just made up this award to lure you guys to the dance, it's already been engraved, so . . ."

The Commander took the trophy. "I'd be honored to accept this Hero of the Year Award. But it doesn't belong to us."

Jetstream nodded. "It belongs to them. The sidekicks. I mean . . . um . . . hero support."

The Commander smiled.

"How about we just call 'em what they really are . . . *heroes*."